Note to Librarians, Teachers, and Parents:

Blastoff! Readers are carefully developed by literacy experts and combine standards-based content with developmentally appropriate text.

Level 1 provides the most support through repetition of high-frequency words, light text, predictable sentence patterns, and strong visual support.

Level 2 offers early readers a bit more challenge through varied simple sentences, increased text load, and less repetition of high-frequency words.

Level 3 advances early-fluent readers toward fluency through increased text and concept load, less reliance on visuals, longer sentences, and more literary language.

Level 4 builds reading stamina by providing more text per page, increased use of punctuation, greater variation in sentence patterns, and increasingly challenging vocabulary.

Level 5 encourages children to move from "learning to read" to "reading to learn" by providing even more text, varied writing styles, and less familiar topics.

Whichever book is right for your reader, Blastoff! Readers are the perfect books to build confidence and encourage a love of reading that will last a lifetime!

This edition first published in 2019 by Bellwether Media, Inc.

No part of this publication may be reproduced in whole or in part without written permission of the publisher. For information regarding permission, write to Bellwether Media, Inc., Attention: Permissions Department, 6012 Blue Circle Drive, Minnetonka, MN 55343.

Library of Congress Cataloging-in-Publication Data

Names: Schuetz, Kari, author.
Title: Monarch Butterfly Migration / by Kari Schuetz.
Description: Minneapolis, MN : Bellwether Media, Inc., 2019. | Series: Blastoff! Readers. Animals on the Move | Audience: Age 5-8. | Audience: Grade K to 3. | Includes bibliographical references and index.
Identifiers: LCCN 2017061804 (print) | LCCN 2018005325 (ebook) | ISBN 9781626178182 (hardcover : alk. paper) | ISBN 9781681035598 (ebook)
Subjects: LCSH: Monarch butterfly--Migration--Juvenile literature.
Classification: LCC QL561.D3 (ebook) | LCC QL561.D3 S24 2019 (print) | DDC 595.78/9--dc23
LC record available at https://lccn.loc.gov/2017061804

Text copyright © 2019 by Bellwether Media, Inc. BLASTOFF! READERS and associated logos are trademarks and/or registered trademarks of Bellwether Media, Inc. SCHOLASTIC, CHILDREN'S PRESS, and associated logos are trademarks and/or registered trademarks of Scholastic Inc., 557 Broadway, New York, NY 10012.

Editor: Paige V. Polinsky   Designer: Jeffrey Kollock

Printed in the United States of America, North Mankato, MN

Table of Contents

Monarch Butterflies	4
High and Dry	8
Day Trips	12
A Relay Finish	18
Glossary	22
To Learn More	23
Index	24

Monarch Butterflies

Monarch butterflies are **insects** known for their long-distance **relay**. Every year, millions of these bright fliers travel with the seasons.

Monarch Butterfly Profile

animal type: insect
habitats: grasslands, forests
size: wingspan: 4 inches (10 centimeters)
weight: 0.01 to 0.03 ounces (0.28 to 0.85 grams)
life span: fall travelers: 8 to 9 months
spring/summer travelers: 2 to 6 weeks

It takes several **generations** to complete the **migration**. The journey covers thousands of miles!

Monarchs have large, light wings to carry them far. **Scales** on these wings help lift the insects during flight.

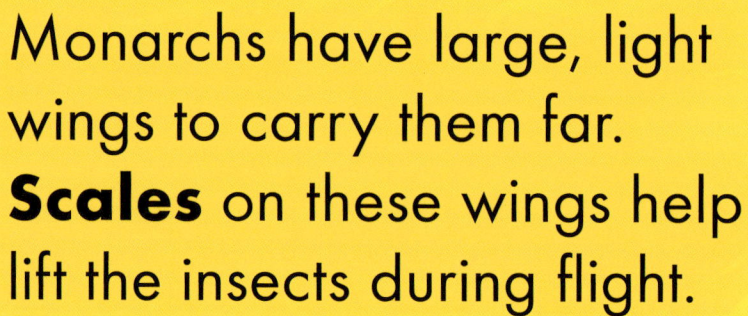
scales

gliding

Tiny hairs all over monarchs' bodies sense the wind's direction and speed. This helps them **glide**.

High and Dry

Monarchs cannot live through northern winters. Winter weather leaves them without food.

The cold also makes their wings too stiff to fly. In fall, the butterflies must head south to stay warm.

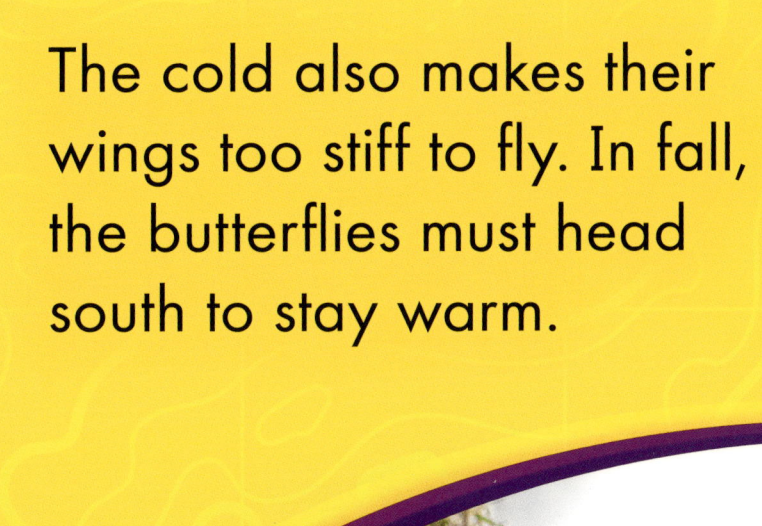

The butterflies need clear skies to travel. Rain makes their wet bodies too heavy to fly. Raindrops can also hurt their thin wings.

On a dry day, the monarchs take flight. They color the sky orange!

Day Trips

Monarchs fly during the daytime. The sun guides their way.

The butterflies glide on the wind. This helps them save energy. They also take breaks on flowers to drink **nectar**.

drinking nectar

Pacific Ocean

The monarchs make it to their southern homes by winter. There, they **roost** in forests.

roosting

Thousands of butterflies can gather in just one tree. They crowd together for extra warmth.

Most **predators** stay away from the roosting monarchs. The butterflies are bright in color to warn that they taste bad.

predator

Still, some birds can eat them without getting sick.

A Relay Finish

milkweed

egg

In spring, monarchs begin the northern migration. Females stop to lay eggs on **milkweed** plants.

Caterpillars then **hatch** from the eggs. They each form a **chrysalis** and become an adult butterfly.

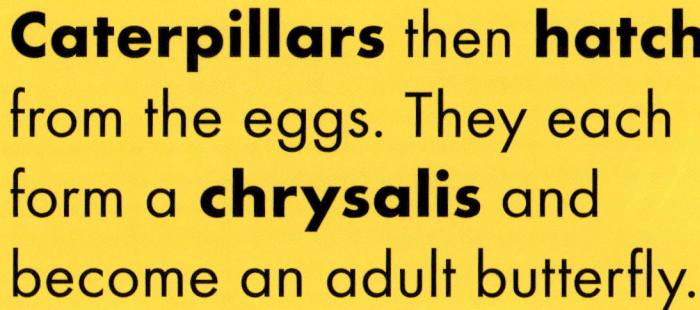

chrysalis

These monarchs live much shorter lives than their parents. They fly as far as they can. Then their children take over the relay.

The butterflies that return north finish the relay started by their great-great-grandparents!

Glossary

caterpillars—wormlike baby monarchs that hatch from eggs

chrysalis—a hard shell that forms around a caterpillar while it changes into a butterfly

generations—groups based on age; a generation is a group of individuals born and living at the same time.

glide—to fly through the air smoothly without flapping wings

hatch—to break out of an egg

insects—small, six-legged animals that have bodies that are divided into three parts

migration—the act of traveling from one place to another, often with the seasons

milkweed—a plant that has a milky juice

nectar—a sweet liquid found in plants, especially flowers

predators—animals that hunt other animals for food

relay—a race completed by a team

roost—to rest in a tree

scales—small, overlapping plates on monarch butterfly wings

To Learn More

AT THE LIBRARY
Fishman, Jon M. *The Monarch Butterfly's Journey*. Minneapolis, Minn.: Lerner Publications, 2018.

Hansen, Grace. *Monarch Butterfly Migration*. Minneapolis, Minn.: Abdo Kids, 2018.

Katz Cooper, Sharon. *When Butterflies Cross the Sky: The Monarch Butterfly Migration*. North Mankato, Minn.: Picture Window Books, 2015.

ON THE WEB
Learning more about monarch butterfly migration is as easy as 1, 2, 3.

1. Go to www.factsurfer.com.

2. Enter "monarch butterfly migration" into the search box.

3. Click the "Surf" button and you will see a list of related web sites.

With factsurfer.com, finding more information is just a click away.

Index

bodies, 7, 10
caterpillars, 19
chrysalis, 19
color, 10, 16
daytime, 12
departure trip, 11
eggs, 18, 19
fall, 9
females, 18
fly, 9, 10, 12, 20
food, 8
generations, 5
glide, 7, 12
hairs, 7
hatch, 19
map, 12-13
mileage, 5, 15
milkweed, 18
nectar, 12
predators, 16, 17

rain, 10
relay, 4, 20
return trip, 20, 21
roost, 14, 16
scales, 6
speed, 7, 15
spring, 18
sun, 12
wind, 7, 12
wings, 6, 9, 10
winters, 8, 14

The images in this book are reproduced through the courtesy of: Annette Shaff, front cover (monarch); Pakhnyushchy, front cover (sky); biletskiy, front cover (grass/flowers); jason Patrick Ross, front cover (gradient map); StevenRussellSmithPhotos, pp. 4-5; Butterfly Hunter, p. 5; Peter Waters, p. 6 (top); Kate Besler, p. 6 (bottom); Seashell317, p. 7; RooM the Agency/ Alamy, p. 8; Francisco J Ramos Gallego, p. 9; JackVandenHeuvel, p. 10; reisegraf.ch, pp. 10-11; Ron Rowan Photography, p. 12; Elizaveta Kirina, p. 14; Noradoa, p. 16; William T Smith, p. 17; Glass and Nature, p. 18 (top); Sari ONeal, p. 18 (bottom); Tommy Daynjer, p. 19; Orchidpoet, p. 20; Sean Xu, pp. 20-21.